Dedication

To Papa Gator and my sweet little hatchlings, Sunny and Violet, thank you for your love, patience and encouragement.

And to the sweet little Nugget we had the privilege of caring for, know that we are honored to have been part of your beginning.

We love you and look forward to the rest of your story.

A Turtle's Tale

Written by
Crystal Henry

Illustrations by
Victoria Samantha Allen

Deep in the Florida swamp Mama Turtle gazed into a hole in the sand
and smiled down at ten beautiful turtle eggs.

Papa Turtle was so proud, and he asked Mama how long until they hatched.

"You have to be patient," she told him.
"Little turtles are worth waiting for."

Papa tried to be patient, but he couldn't wait to snuggle his baby turtles.
He loved Mama Turtle very much, and he was ready to complete their family.

"I'll try to be patient," Papa said.

Mama smiled and began to cover her nest.

An osprey flew overhead, and Mama Turtle looked up.
A storm was brewing in the distance.

Papa began to worry.

That night, as Mama and Papa Turtle slept, a great hurricane swelled off the coast.

As it approached, hard rains flooded the swampland, and great winds
brought the mighty cypress trees crashing to the ground.

Mama did her best to protect her nest, but she and Papa
were swept away with the wind and rain.

The nest and the ten beautiful turtle eggs were lost in the storm.

The next morning Mama and Papa Turtle went searching for their nest,
but the storm had devastated the swamp.

They were so far from home.

Mama Turtle cried big turtle tears, but Papa told her not to give up.

They would find their family.

She would just have to be patient.

On the other side of the swamp Mother and Father Gator
cruised through the water looking for their own babies.
They too were separated in the storm, and Mother Gator was worried sick.
Snip and Snap were still hatchlings, and they needed looking after.
What would become of her babies without their mother?

Just then she heard a rustle on the river bank.
As Mother Gator peered through the fetterbush she saw Snip and Snap
giggling and nudging two small white balls back and forth.
Mother Gator wept for joy upon seeing her babies safe and sound.

"Come here my little loves!"
Mother Gator cried.
But Snip and Snap were too busy
playing to notice her return.
"What do you have there,"
Father Gator asked.

Mother Gator looked closely and said,
"Why it's two snapping turtle eggs. The storm must have upset their nest."
"Alright Snip, leave it alone and let's go," said Father Gator.
"Snap, you too. We don't have any business with snapping turtle eggs."

But Mother Gator couldn't help but wonder what would become of these lonely little eggs.
"Father dear," she said.
"Why don't we look after the eggs?
Just for a few days until their mother comes back."

Father Gator chomped his teeth and sank under water to think.
Mother went under too and nudged his long green snout.
"Remember when our babies were lost?" she asked.
"If Mama Turtle had found them what would you have her do?"

Father looked at Snip and Snap nudging the little eggs back and forth across the muddy bank.
"You're right," he said.
"But let's not just float around here like bumps on a log. Let's go try to find their nest."

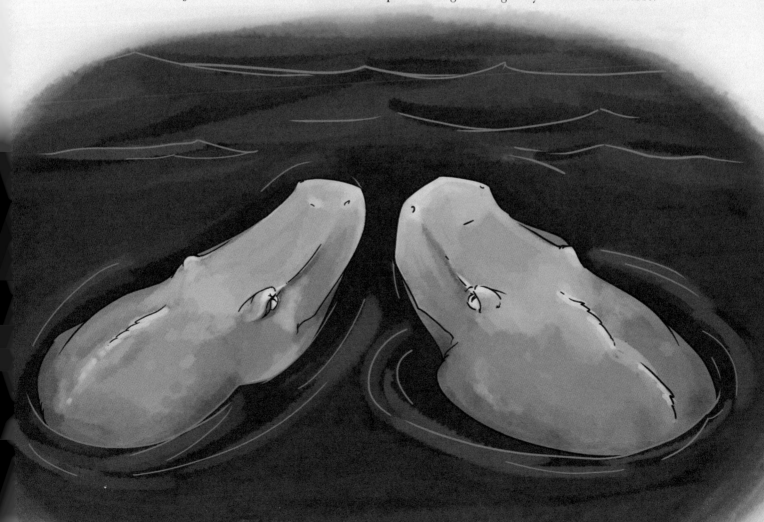

So Mother and Father Gator along with Snip and Snap began their journey
with the little eggs to the turtle nesting grounds.

Meanwhile Mama and Papa Turtle were slowly making their way back home.

"I wouldn't know what to do with baby turtles anyway,"
Mama Turtle sighed as she trudged slowly through the muddy swamp.

"Nonsense," Papa Turtle said.
"Turtles have been having turtle babies since the dawn of time.
You'll know what to do when you see them."

"If I see them," Mama Turtle said.
A great big turtle tear rolled down her little muddy cheek.

Days passed as the two families trudged across the swamp in search of the turtle nests.

Mother Gator nudged the tiny eggs carefully across the soft ground with her snout, but it was not easy.

"Maybe you should try carrying the eggs," Father Gator said.

"Carry them?" squawked an egret flying overhead.

"Who ever heard of a gator caring for a turtle egg?"

"Oh never mind that old bird," Father said. "Go ahead. We have to cross the river to get to the nesting grounds."

Mother Gator gently took the eggs into her mouth and carefully lowered herself into the water.

Snip and Snap swam right next to Mother, and Father followed closely behind.

The whole Gator family was on a mission to save those eggs.

Just then, the Gators heard a loud buzzing sound.

Mother looked up just in time to see a swamp boat barreling straight toward them.

She needed help getting Snip and Snap to safety, but as she opened her mouth to yell,
the eggs fell to the bottom of the river.

Father saw the boat too.
He swept Snip and Snap up onto his back just in time and dove under the water.

The boat flew by overhead, and he popped back to the surface to make
sure Mother Gator and the eggs were okay.

He saw her climbing on the river bank, and he swam quickly to meet her.

"I lost an egg!" Mother Gator cried.
"I have to go back and find it."

Mother and Father Gator searched and searched underwater
while Snip and Snap carefully guarded the lone turtle egg on the river bank.

The Gators looked all around, but the little
egg had been carried away in the current.

The Gator family sadly trudged on with the
last of the turtle eggs toward the nesting grounds.

When they arrived, Mother Gator asked
Father, Snip and Snap to stay by the bank so they didn't scare the turtles.

Snip and Snap grumbled, but Father swept them back with his tail.

As Mother approached the turtle nests she saw two sullen turtles
staring down into an empty hole in the sand.

Mother Gator put the egg down gently and cleared her throat.

"Whoa!"
Papa Turtle flipped clean over into the hole
when he saw the big gator staring straight at him.

"Sorry!"
Mother Gator said as she nudged the egg with her nose.
"I was wondering if you know who this belongs to."

"My egg!" Mama Turtle cried.
"You found my egg! My baby turtle!"

Papa Turtle rolled back over, and as fast
as a turtle can he scrambled out of the hole.

He got to the egg just as it started to wiggle.

The egg began to open, and a tiny
turtle head peeked out of the shell.

The baby turtle blinked and the
first thing she saw was big Mother Gator
staring down with her toothy grin.

The baby turtle smiled and peered around.
When she saw Mama Turtle's face she
burst from her shell.

"Mama!" she croaked.

"My baby," Mama Turtle said softly.

Papa Turtle came and snuggled his baby turtle
for the very first time.

They found their family at last.

"Thank you," Mama Turtle said to Mother Gator with big turtle tears in her eyes.
"I can't believe you would go through all this trouble for one tiny turtle egg."

"I am a mama," Mother Gator said.
"And I know what it is like to lose a baby."

Just then Snip and Snap came crashing through the
swamp grass followed by big Father Gator.

"I'm sorry!" Father Gator said as he chased the two tiny gators.
"They just wanted to see the egg one more time."

"It's too late," Mother Gator said. "The egg is gone."

Snip and Snap squeaked and croaked in protest...
until they saw the baby turtle.

Snip and Snap crawled carefully
over to the tiny turtle and
gently nudged her with
their gator noses.

The little turtle giggled
and snapped playfully.

"Can we keep her Mother?
Can we?"
the young gators asked.

"No dears. Our job was
to deliver her safely,"
Mother Gator said.
"She belongs with her mother
just as you belong with me."

The baby gators nuzzled their
mother as the little turtle
crawled slowly to hers.

"You were right,"
Papa Turtle said to Mama
as he gently kissed his baby.

"Little turtles are worth
waiting for."

The End

Crystal Henry is a freelance writer glad to be back in her native Texas land. She is a University of Florida alumna who stays true to her Florida writing roots through her work with Our Town Magazine and her award-winning column, Naked Salsa. She is a boobs out breastfeeding advocate and semi-crunchy mom whose work has been featured on sites such as Scary Mommy, eHow, LIVESTRONG and ModernMom.

Her world-domination-smart husband and two hilariously inappropriate little girls constantly provide fodder for her column and #preschoolproblems blog. But having two newborns of her own broke the baby fever that once burned deep within her. And instead she rents out her oven to another woman's bun and documents her surrogacy journey with humor and honesty through her blog, Her Eggs My Basket.

Victoria Samantha Allen is a 2015 graduate of Savannah College of Art and Design (SCAD, Savannah) with a BFA in Illustration. This past year she has traveled extensively and most recently worked in New York. Her work and love of children's books continues after this charming turtle's tale, as she is currently writing and illustrating her own series. She currently lives in her native Louisiana.

Made in the USA
Middletown, DE
05 March 2022

62194370R00015